To Kristen, with love—
*"With one note the nightingale*
*indicates the rose" (Rumi)*
—S. C.

Henry Holt and Company, LLC
*Publishers since 1866*
115 West 18th Street
New York, New York 10011
www.henryholt.com

Henry Holt is a registered trademark of Henry Holt and Company, LLC
Copyright © 2004 by Stephen Costanza
All rights reserved.
Distributed in Canada by H. B. Fenn and Company Ltd.

Library of Congress Catalog Card Number: 2003020998
Full Library of Congress Cataloging-in-Publication Data available at http://catalog.loc.gov/

ISBN 0-8050-6627-6 / EAN 978-0-8050-6627-2
First Edition—2004 / Designed by Patrick Collins
The artist used gouache, acrylic, and colored pencil on illustration board
to create the illustrations for this book.
Printed in the United States of America on acid-free paper. ∞

1  3  5  7  9  10  8  6  4  2

# Mozart Finds a Melody

## Stephen Costanza

*Stephen Costanza*

Henry Holt and Company

New York

O n a fine spring day in the Imperial Austrian city of Vienna, Wolfgang Amadeus Mozart glanced at the clock against the wall and sighed a great, long SIGH.

"Goodness me," he said. "I must compose a new piano concerto to be performed this Saturday evening. Here it is Monday already, and I can't think of a single note!"

For the first time in Wolfgang's life, the famous composer was at a loss for a tune. He tried every trick to get his imagination going. He sang standing on his head.

He played his violin in the bathtub.

He even threw darts at the blank music paper, hoping that the holes would form an interesting melody on the staff lines. Alas, nothing worked.

"Oh dear," he said. "What on earth am I going to do?"

Just then, Wolfgang's pet starling, Miss Bimms, was waking from her afternoon nap and feeling very hungry. She sat up straight on her perch, shook her tail feathers a couple of times, and noticing that her bird feeder was empty, said, *"Chirp, chirp, chiiirp."*

"Hmmm," said Wolfgang, looking up at the bird and rubbing his chin. "Not bad."

*"Chirp, chirp, chirp-chiirrp-chirp,"* said Miss Bimms, getting quite hungry.

"Yes, yes, that was lovely!" said Wolfgang, and he started scribbling down some notes.

*"CHIRP, CHIRP, CHIRRRP-CHIRRRP-CHIRRRRRRRP,"* cried birdie, falling off her perch.

"That's it!" shouted Wolfgang, jumping out of his chair. He danced a little jig on his way to the fortepiano, where he played the starling's melody. And what a fine melody it was, seventeen notes in all.

"Bravo, bravo, a thousand bravos!" said Mozart between giggles. "The perfect beginning for my piano concerto. And I have you to thank, Kapellmeister Bimms. Together we shall finish the concerto, and—oh! How careless of me. There's no birdseed in your feeder. Well now, we can't compose on an empty stomach. Lunch is served!"

Wolfgang grabbed some birdseed, opened the cage door, and said, "First, a thousand kisses from your humble friend." He closed his eyes and puckered his lips, but poor Miss Bimms, unaccustomed as she was to being kissed, flew out of Wolfgang's hands and fluttered about the room.

And the more she flew, the more alarmed she became.
She fluttered under the fortepiano, then flitted about
the ceiling, after which she swooped under the
desk chair, changed directions, and darted
straight out the window.

"Miss Bimms," cried Wolfgang.
But the starling flew farther
and farther away in great lopsided
circles and appeared smaller and
smaller and smaller.

"I must find her!" cried Wolfgang.
"How else will I be able to finish my
concerto?" He seized the birdcage,
threw on his topcoat, put some
birdseed into his pocket, and
stepped outside . . .

. . . to the street below.

Now Wolfgang's apartment was located right on the Graben, which stood next to the Kohlmarkt, one of the busiest, brightest, and gayest of streets in all Vienna. Walking a few paces, the composer cleared his throat and cupped his hands to his mouth.

"Here, birdie, birdie, birdie," sang Wolfgang. "Come to me, my plumed little nubbin. My little beaked bagatelle, my feathered little chirrrpy."

The good people of Vienna pretended not to notice the little man with the birdcage, but some couldn't refrain from pointing and talking among themselves. "Surely Mozart has gone mad," they whispered.

"Oh dear, this will be much harder than I thought," said Wolfgang, looking all around for his pet friend. He whistled the starling's melody. "What a charming tune she has given me."

Soon enough, Wolfgang came upon Herr Schafle
the baker and, catching him in the window of his shop,
asked, "Excuse me, Herr Schafle, have you seen my pet
starling? She's about this big. I need her to help me finish
my piano concerto."

The baker was about as simple as they come, and
after hearing Wolfgang's story, he decided to play a
joke on him.

"Why, of course I saw your starling, but unfortunately
I didn't know it belonged to you. I am sorry to report
that I baked the bird in a pie only ten minutes ago."

And with that, Herr Schafle was so pleased with
himself that he let out a long, deep laugh.

*"Ha-ha-ha-ha-ha-ha-ha-ha-ha-ha-ha-ha-ha!"*

Acknowledging the baker's wisecrack, Wolfgang rolled his eyes, headed straight for the door, then abruptly stopped in his tracks.

"Hmmm," he thought, scratching his ear. "Not bad."

"*Ha-ha-ha-ha-ha-ha-ha-ha-ha-ha-ha-ha-ha!*" bellowed Herr Schafle, and the more he roared, the redder he became.

"Yes, yes, that was lovely," Wolfgang replied, and he scribbled down some notes. "A little more vibrato, if you please, Herr Schafle."

Indeed, the shop began to shake at its very foundation, and the baker was so beside himself that he had to leave the room.

"My, these basses will do very nicely," said Wolfgang, looking at the page. "Thank you, Herr Schafle! Good day."

And through the city continued Wolfgang, calling out for Miss Bimms. He searched high and low for his dear friend, scattering birdseed along the way. And as he whistled the starling's melody, the sounds of the street began to play in his ears.

The rattle of carriage wheels mingled with the
squawks of geese and the barking of dogs; the hum in
the coffeehouses kept perfect time with the clanging
of church bells. The entire town came alive with
musical possibilities, and it all went into his score.

Saturday evening arrived, and with a few hours to spare for rehearsal, Wolfgang finished the concerto. Relieved though he was, he worried about his little companion and remembered how she helped bring his inspiration back. "I shall dedicate this to dear Miss Bimms," said Wolfgang, and he wrote his inscription on the front page of the score.

Finally the concert was about to begin, and in no finer place than the Burgtheater, the most splendid concert hall in the land. Wolfgang stepped onto the stage and bowed to the audience. Taking his place at the fortepiano, he turned to the orchestra with his hand in the air, and all fell silent.

A brilliant chord in G major rang out of the theater and rushed into the moonlit sky. A soft breeze shifted the notes before they climbed steadily higher, and up, up, up rose the magnificent harmonies of Wolfgang's concerto. Over the city the music soared, past the Kohlmarkt, beyond the Graben, even above the steeple at Saint Stephen's Cathedral, the highest point in all Vienna.

And there, hiding from the cold and shivering from beak to tail, was Miss Bimms herself.

Now, whether you have wings or not, the top of this particular cathedral is no place for anyone, especially if you're a hungry starling who has lost her way and has a cold into the bargain.

Miss Bimms was about to sneeze, when suddenly she became very still. Was that singing she heard, or perhaps the wind? She stretched her neck out a little farther, straining to hear the familiar sound as it floated past her. Yes, indeed it was—she recognized her melody! And with that, Miss Bimms summoned all her remaining strength and leaped into the night air. First to the left she flew, losing the sound before curving to the right, then straight ahead as the music grew louder and louder. Past the Kohlmarkt, beyond the Graben, the music growing louder still, until at last she swooped down upon the roof of the Burgtheater and crept inside an open window.

Flapping her tired wings as best she could, Miss Bimms made her way to the upper balcony (not before ruffling a few feathers). She then took a deep breath and began to sing.

The orchestra stopped as all assembled turned to listen to Miss Bimms. She sang the melody of the concerto, and her little voice filled the entire Burgtheater. When she was finished, she dove off the balcony and landed right on Wolfgang's baton.

"Miss Bimms!" cried Wolfgang.

"Achoo," replied Miss Bimms.

"My, we need to take care of that cold right away," whispered Wolfgang. "A warm cup of tea with honey and some fresh cracked corn for you, as soon as we get home." He then raised his arm, and the orchestra began to play once more, this time with both Wolfgang and Miss Bimms conducting.

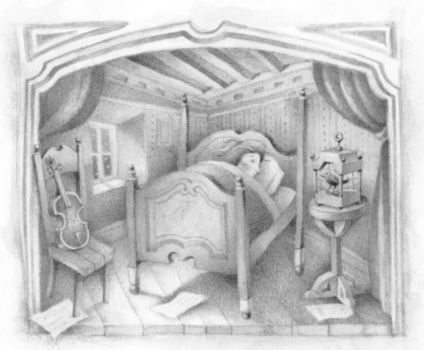

Later that evening, after a cup of hot chamomile
tea, Miss Bimms hopped back on her favorite perch,
shook her tail feathers a couple of times, and settled
down for a good night's rest. Wolfgang tiptoed up to the
birdcage and, puckering his lips, softly whistled the starling's
melody. Soon one voice joined the other, and as their chirping
and singing and chiming filled the room, a finer duet between two
friends was never heard. At last Miss Bimms slowly closed her eyes
as they reached the finale. Wolfgang checked the latch on the
birdcage door, and before long he too was fast asleep.

# Author's Note

My affinity for Mozart's music began at a live performance of *Amadeus*, when, as the lush harmonies seemed to rise from the stage and flood the theater with sound, I sat electrified in my chair, transported to another world. Before that experience I had only a casual regard for classical music; even less so for Mozart. I loved the piano, however. Having started lessons at age twelve, I was immediately captivated with ragtime and became a devotee, later performing rags professionally with a violinist friend for several years. But much of Mozart's music eluded me, until that one night in the theater.

Since then I have pored over countless scores by Mozart and devoured much information about his life and times, both legendary and factual. The idea for *Mozart Finds a Melody* originated with one such fact. Among the animals owned by Mozart were a fox terrier, a canary, and a starling. Apparently the starling was especially musical and, to Mozart's delight, had learned to sing almost to perfection the first few bars of the final theme from his Piano Concerto no. 17 in G Major. After hearing the starling, Mozart wrote in his account book, "That was lovely." When the starling died in 1787, he wrote a eulogy for his winged companion. I took the name of Miss Bimms from the fox terrier, which the Mozart family variously called Pimperl, Bimperl, or Miss Bimbes.

While creating the illustrations for this book, I found myself at times not unlike Mozart, standing with empty birdcage in hand and hoping to win back his departed muse. Yet my greatest joys came as I discovered, like Mozart, that what seems lost is never really far away—and how a community of friends can sustain one's spirit and help bring an idea to fruition.